C000156915

CONT.

FREEDOM OVER ME

THE NINE LIVES OF GABRIELLE: FOR THREE SHE STRAYS - BOOK 3

LAURA MARIANI

the
PEOPLE
ALCHEMIST

ABOUT THE AUTHOR

Laura Mariani is an Author, Speaker and Entrepreneur.

She started her consulting business after a successful career as Senior HR Director within global brands in FMCG, Retail, Media and Pharma.

Laura is incredibly passionate about helping other women to break through barriers limiting their personal and/or professional fulfilment.

Her best selling nonfiction *STOP IT! It is all in your head* and the *THINK, LOOK & ACT THE PART* series have been described as success and transformation 101.

She is a Fellow of the Chartered Institute of Personnel & Development (FCIPD), Fellow of the Australian Human Resources Institute (FAHRI), Fellow of the Institute of Leadership & Management (FInstLM), Member of the Society of Human Resources Management (SHRM) and Member of the Change Institute.

She is based in London, England with a strong penchant for travel and visiting new places. She is a food lover, ballet fanatic, passionate about music, art, theatre. She likes painting and drawing (for self-expression not selling but hey, you never know…), tennis, rugby, and of course fashion (the Pope is Catholic after all).

www.thepeoplealchemist.com
@PeopleAlchemist
instagram.com/lauramariani_author

NEW FICTION OUT ON 12 JULY

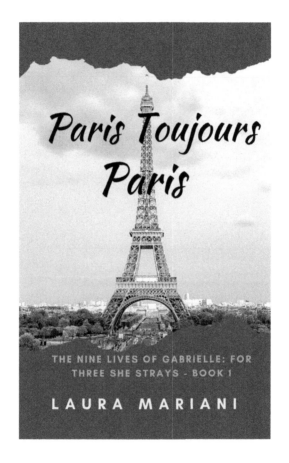

Paris Toujours Paris

THE NINE LIVES OF GABRIELLE: FOR
THREE SHE STRAYS - BOOK 1

LAURA MARIANI

THE NINE LIVES OF GABRIELLE: FOR
THREE SHE STRAYS - BOOK 2

ME MYSELF *and Us*

LAURA MARIANI

NEW NON-FICTION BY LAURA MARIANI

INCREDIBLY INSPIRING!
A BOOK PERFECT FOR WOMEN IN BUSINESS.

90 DAYS TO REBOOT YOUR CAREER

*How to reinvent yourself,
your career and your life*

BY LAURA MARIANI

ALSO BY LAURA MARIANI

Fiction

For Three She Plays - Book 1 - 3

A New York Adventure

Troubled after the break-up of a long term relationship, Gabrielle sets out for a sabbatical in New York.

A travelogue searching for self, pleasure and fun. And the Big Apple doesn't disappoint.

Searching for Goren

Why are we always choosing people who don't allow intimacy? Is it because deep down we don't want it?

Tasting Freedom

As her trip to New York comes to an end, her shackles bare falling and Gabrielle begins to taste, finally, freedom.

Non-Fiction

STOP IT! It is all in your head

The RULE BOOK to Smash The infamous glass ceiling -

For women & young women everywhere - personal transformation & success 101.

The Think, Look & Act The Part Series.

Think The Part

Upgrade your consciousness and mind-set.

Make winning a key part of your life and business.

Look The Part

Upgrade your personal brand.

Make presenting your unique Best Self a key part of your life and business.

Act The Part

A personal coach to act in spite of fear, right here, right now.

More non-fiction books and courses are coming soon. For new releases, giveaways and pre-release specials check www. thepeoplealchemist.com

You can also buy my books and courses directly from me at www. payhip.com/LauraMariani

FREEDOM OVER ME

The Global annual meeting had ended; it had been an astounding success, especially for Gabrielle.

People commented on how different this year had been, more inclusive, more fitting of a multi-billion euros global company, a leader in its field, rather than a provincial French company. Tradition and heritage had the rightful place in the strategy.

Everybody appreciated the changes and felt the company was also starting to speak their language.

It was a bittersweet victory for Gabrielle, professionally elating but personally devastating.

Le PDG tried desperately to reach her, to talk to her. He had to explain. Gabrielle had to know.

"*Madame, pour Vous*", the concierge said whilst she was checking out of the hotel and handed over a letter.

"*Merci*," she said and settled the bill.

Looking at her handwritten name on the envelope, she knew it was from him. But she didn't open it whilst on the train back to Paris, too many people she knew around.

·   ·   ·

She was going back to London from there for a well-deserved long weekend; there, on the Eurostar, with a glass of some kind of liquor in her hand, she started reading:

"Dear Gabrielle,

Don't be afraid of how much I desire you. I will shield you with love the next time I see you, with kisses and caresses.

I want to dive with you in all the pleasures of the flesh so that you faint.

I want you to be astounded by me and admit that you have never dreamed of such things possible ...."

Tears were streaming down her cheeks.

".......You have raised new hope and fun in me, and I love you...."

"*Madame, are you OK?*" asked the very attentive server on the train. They didn't often see many people crying their hearts out in business class.

"I'm good, thank you. Thanks for asking", Gabrielle replied.

"All this madness I asked of you, I know there is confusion in your silence — but there are no actual words to describe my great love...." she continued reading.

"Last night I dreamed about you ...... I was you. You were me.

Then, we caught fire. I remember I was smothering the fire with my shirt. But you were a different, a shadow, as drawn with chalk, and you were lifeless, fading away from me.

Please don't leave me, my darling Gabrielle. I am nothing without you."

I'm yours forever."

"Yes, forever mine, forever hers", she thought. It was the longest two and half hours of her life.

She spent the next twenty-four hours in bed. She couldn't be bothered doing anything, going anywhere. *Le PDG's* letter clutched in her hands.

Gabrielle was feeling both aching for him and repulsed at the same time.

. . .

She hadn't spoken to him yet. He called her numerous times, but she didn't pick up. She let the calls go to voicemail every time. He texted her a myriad of times, and she didn't respond either.

Ring, ring …. ring ring …

Her mobile was buzzing.

"Ciao bella", the voice said "bentornata". It was Paola, her trusted friend, checking in on her.

"Hiya", Gabrielle replied. They chatted for a while, she really wanted to be left alone, but she knew her friend was trying to jerk her out of her apathy.

"Cicci, lunch on Sunday", Paola said.

It wasn't a question, and she wouldn't have taken no for an answer anyway.

"I'll come to Islington, and we'll go somewhere in your area".

Gabrielle knew it was pointless arguing or saying no; she would have shown up at her house anyway. Paola knew how to shake her up when she needed it.

• • •

"Remember to bring your passport when you are travelling from the suburbs", Gabrielle said, with their longstanding joke about Paola living in Richmond.

"I'll try. See you Sunday", she said.

Sunday came quicker than she realised, et voilà, it was soon time to meet Paola for a good catch-up.

Paola, her no-nonsense Italian friend who she had known since she had arrived in London.

Paola managed not to lose her strong accent after almost twenty years in the country. She always made Gabrielle smile.

The weather was warming up, and they were looking for somewhere to eat with outside space. Londoners turn into mini lizards and seek the sun whenever it seems like it is coming out.

Ultimately, they opted for The Alwyne Castle, a charming pub in Islington with a beer garden, situated only a minute's walk from Highbury & Islington underground station.

The Alwyne has lots of space, especially outside, which is ideal for building a suntan and carries a good beer and wine selection.

· · ·

They met for an early Sunday lunch; Gabrielle definitely needed some cheering before heading back to Paris.

"Hello ladies", said the waiter ", a table outside or inside?".
   "Outside, outside", they replied in unison.

They both glanced at the menu and quickly chose: beef carpaccio and seared scallops, perfectly done and seasoned for starter and the obligatory Sunday Roast (obviously).

"Any drinks while you are waiting?"

Gabrielle and Paola looked at each other and said, "A bottle of house red and sparkling water, thanks".

"So, *ciccia mia*, what's going on?" Paola started as soon as the waiter had left their table.

It had been a while since they last saw each other, and they had a lot to talk about.

Gabrielle, slowly and softly, started to tell her story: her first meeting with *Le PDG*, their clandestine meetings anywhere and everywhere, and, to finish, she recounted what just happened in *Londrienne* at the global annual conference.

· · ·

"Seared scallops?" the server interrupted.

"Me", Paola raised her hand.

"Ciccia, ciccia, no no no ..." Paola went on after he had served them with their starters.

"But, but you are having an affair too," Gabrielle responded, baffled.

Paola had been married to an Englishman for the last ten years, and they had two gorgeous daughters. She loved them all dearly; however, she had kept her bit on the side: an Italian lover Paola met from time to time when visiting her mother every couple of months.

"*La differenza mia cara*, for me it's just sex.

I tell Marco I'm going over; if he is available, we meet; if he isn't, it is still OK, like a 'human vibrator' on call. Nothing else. He knows how to make me come, and he does his job.

He doesn't want or need anything more from me and me from him".

Her husband lacked a bit in the sex drive department and was happy to go without it. Paola wasn't.

. . .

Martin was an outstanding father and husband; she would never leave him, but needs were needs.

"*Tu ciccia mia,* are getting involved. No, correction, you are involved emotionally.

Plus, you feel guilty even when you find money on the pavement, or someone gives you extra change in shops. Remember that time you went back to return ten pence? Ten pence. And now you are having an affair with a married man?" she paused, shaking her head.

"No, no, no, not for you. I can read guilt splattered all over your face; it is consuming you".

The main course arrived; Gabrielle was impressed that they managed to handle the timing of the two orders with no problem, especially considering she liked her beef still muuuing and rare whilst her friend liked it almost cremated.

The beef was delicious, and the beef dripping roast potatoes were perfectly cooked.

Gabrielle knew Paola was right. But she couldn't bear to stop it yet.

· · ·

"Relationships aren't easy," she thought, "they take a different take because the memories and stories can transform during crucial moments", she was illuding herself.

Finally, they ended the meal with the British Cheeseboard washed down with more red.

"*Se hai bisogno, lo sai che sono qui*", Paola said.
   "I know".

At 6.00 am on Monday morning, Gabrielle started to get ready to leave the house. The first Eurostar to Paris was at 7.00 am, and St Pancras station was not that far from her home; she had plenty of time.

The two and half hours seemed to pass by incredibly slowly. It felt more like a lifetime.

On the one hand, she was glad. But, on the other hand, she wasn't really looking forward to seeing him again. Gabrielle was postponing the inevitable, and she had to meet him sometime. She was working directly for him, after all.

Until meeting *Le PDG,* Gabrielle's life experience was mainly secondhand, observed, and never viscerally involved. And now that her layers are slowly peeling away, and all the emotions she had repressed for so long, jealousy, frustration, and anger were coming to the surface.

•   •   •

All her life, she had been a closet bohemian. She always loved to live big, outrageously. Outside she was the perfect daughter and businesswoman but inside, she had always been Isadora Duncan.

She wanted a life outside the bell curve and to suck the marrow out of life. But she wanted people to like her too…
And so, she conformed.

Gabrielle arrived at the office after 11.00 am. People were still buzzing from the conference; she noticed *Le PDG* was not in.

"Good", she thought. She preferred it that away, at least today.

The day went by, and she had meetings back to back, so she had no time to think.

She left the office a bit late but decided to walk home anyway. Even though it was a bit far from *Tour Montparnasse* to the right behind *Gare Du Nord*, she needed the fresh air.

When she arrived at her building, he was standing there. *Le PDG*. He was holding a bouquet of purple hyacinths in his hands, and one single red rose.

"I'm sorry", he said. "I should have told you myself. I took for granted that you knew about the gossip mill like everyone else seems to.

. . .

"I can't stop thinking about you. Please don't leave me. I am nothing without you."

And there he was, standing right in front of the building entrance; she couldn't get in without acknowledging his presence one way or the other.

She didn't want to, but she was aching for him.

"There has been no other since I met you. Only you", he continued.

"Did you get my letter?" he asked. Gabrielle nodded.

And suddenly, they were making love in her apartment, on the floor, on the table, starving for each other. They stayed up all night; it was the first time he had stayed over.

And from then on, it became more regular. Le PDG was scared of losing Gabrielle and was trying his best to reassure her.

She wasn't one of the many other women, but the other woman nevertheless.

. . .

Relationships aren't easy; they take a different take because of the memories and stories transformed during crucial moments.

Gabrielle had decided to stop commuting for a bit and fully experience Paris. At least for a while. She had to give Paris the attention and love it deserved.

"Paris is always a good idea", Audrey Hepburn said.

"Indeed, it is Audrey. Indeed it is." And even though summer in France meant a looooong holiday for the French who escaped to the coast or family house, it was worthed.

Gabrielle enjoyed walking around Paris and taking in the open-air architectural views, which were even more breathtaking with the sunshine.

"Summer brings out the best in Paris", she thought, "long days and nights when you can enjoy walking out and about, stunning views, sipping cocktails on terraces and dining al fresco".

Her Paris apartment was small and without outside space but there were many gorgeous parks in Paris she could enjoy:

big ones (*Bois de Vincennes, Bois de Boulogne, Buttes-Chaumont, Parc Floral, Parc de la Villette*),

elegant ones (*Palais-Royal, Jardin du Luxembourg, Jardins des Plantes*), and the in-between (*Parc Monceau, Parc Montsouris*).

All very charming and hosting various summer events that pair well with picnic time, and Gabrielle took full advantage of them.

Le PDG sometimes stayed at the weekend, and they relished watching the occasional movie in the *Parc de la Villette,* where there is a month-long *Cinema en Plein Air festival* with the city's most gigantic movie screen.

It was perfect, almost idyllic: some delicious food and a bottle of wine watching a movie whilst the sun set - the illusion of a proper relationship.

With or without *Le PDG* though, Gabrielle wanted to enjoy Paris, sometimes taking a tour alone from a boat on the Seine.

A tour on *Les Bateaux Mouches* lasts approximately two and six hours and offers great sightseeing with commentary with plenty of Champagne. Or a meal served on exquisite white linen.

She deserved to experience all of it.

She loved how, in the summer, Paris becomes a seaside resort and welcomes *Paris Plages* in the new *Parc Rives de Seine*, with sun loungers and palm trees popping up just by the water's edge.

Plus, every boutique and department store in Paris has super anticipated sales *soldes d'été*.

She was squeezing in as much as she could as if she knew ...

Summer came and went, and the relationship with *Le PDG* became more stable, almost routine, and predictable.

It was as if they had sucked the marrow out, and now only the bones were left behind, holding the skeleton up. Nevertheless, he was still her addiction.

Gabrielle realised that she had now been in Paris, in her position for almost a year.

"Career progression is slow in Paris", she had been thinking.

"Somehow, people stay in the same position much longer than in the UK, where everyone expects to be promoted or move every couple of years".

She was feeling restless but wasn't quite sure why.

. . .

Her role was keeping her very busy with regular travel to the different branches of the company worldwide. Christmas was just around the corner.

She was away from the office more and more, and working from home started to creep in. From the London home.

She started commuting again and travelling back on Thursdays more regularly.

And then, just like that, everything changed ...

On Monday, 23 March 2020, the Prime Minister announced the first lockdown in the UK, ordering people to stay at home. And on 26 March, the lockdown measures legally came into force. Gabrielle was stuck in London.

Life can turn just in a second. Just like that. All the things you always wanted to do on pause. Until someone else decides to press the play button again.

Tomorrow, always longing for tomorrow, and suddenly, there almost wasn't a tomorrow.

Gabrielle kept in touch with the office, making great use of Teams and Zoom and continued working.

. . .

To be fair, she enjoyed being back in her home and the alone time.

She had always been a loner: a child lost in her books, as an adult chasing the next win in the never-ending climb.

She had cancelled many events before, dates, and meetings with friends at the last minute.

There was always tomorrow. There was always something more important to do.

But, after a while, her body and brain started fighting themselves. They were fighting her or something.

She felt exhausted all the time, and all the energy was wiped out of her. She was so fatigued that she was struggling to complete even the most minor tasks. And yet, Gabrielle was unable to get any rest.

She tested to see if she had caught the dreaded C, but no, she hadn't.

Her body was on fire. And on top of throbbing soreness, she was experiencing pins-and-needles sensation prickling throughout.

· · ·

Her mind went into overdrive to the point where she was feeling paranoid, irritable and moody. She couldn't stay still for even a moment.

She couldn't understand what was happening to her.

After a few months, with the physical symptoms subsiding, she was starting to see things clearly again.

She had been withdrawing from the most potent drug.

Overall, the various lockdowns and consequent restrictions had been good for her, a time to focus on herself with little distraction.

And now, after the 'detox', she was getting to know who Gabrielle actually was or wanted to be.

Fully and unapologetically. Isadora Duncan and all.
    And levelling up big time.

The pandemic gave Gabrielle a new, more in-depth appreciation of being out there, alone, in gratitude for life. Appreciating everything that she was so lucky to be able to experience.

·   ·   ·

Sometimes it takes a great emergency or crisis to delve deep and discover how much more you can do. Or should do.

Gabrielle had never been afraid to make big choices: she left her big corporate job, Paris and *Le PDG*, in the middle of the pandemic.

Everybody thought she was crazy. But she knew it was the right thing to do.

She wanted to take her time to figure out what she really wanted. And so she reconnected with her inner Isadora and reprised some childhood passion, and started writing and illustrating children's books and a YouTube channel / podcast.

She also began to treat her body and herself with more love and kindness, no more torture and self-flagellation with super hard schedules. Or self-destructive affairs. Nothing left to prove.

She liked this Gabrielle. And this Gabrielle had attracted the most wonderful man.

She had to make sure that Mr Wonderful knew that THE letter he was holding in his hands was only a page in the book of her life, a chapter fully closed, and she was waiting to continue writing her story with him, and only him.

. . .

For Gabrielle had played, had strayed,
   and now she was ready to stay.

… Because the greatest love of all
Is happening to me
I found the greatest love of all
Inside of me
The greatest love of all
Is easy to achieve
Learning to love yourself
It is the greatest love of all

---

songwriters: **Linda Creed , Michael Masser**

DISCLAIMER

Freedom Over Me is a work of fiction.

Although its form is that of a semi-autobiography (Gabrielle's) it is not one.

With the exception of public places, any resemblance to persons living or dead is coincidental. Space and time have been rearranged to suit the convenience of the book, memory has its own story to tell.

The opinions expressed are those of the characters and should not be confused with the author's.

AUTHOR'S NOTE

Thank you so much for reading *Freedom Over Me*.

I hope you enjoyed this novellas as a form of escapism, but perhaps you also glimpsed something beneath as you read. A review would be much appreciated as it helps other readers discover the story. Thanks.

If you sign up for my newsletter you'll be notified of giveaways, new releases and receive personal updates from behind the scenes of my business and books.

Go to www.thepeoplealchemist.com to get started.

Places in the book

I have set the story in real places in Paris and in a modelled fictional town in the north of France for *Le PDG* backstory. You can see some of the places/mentions here:

- Bois de Vincennes
- Bois de Boulogne,

- Buttes-Chaumont
- Canonbury Square and Gardens
- Cinema en Plein Air festival
- Eurostar
- Gare du Nord
- Highbury & Islington
- Jardin du Luxembourg
- Jardins des Plantes
- Le Metro
- Parc Rives de Seine
- Paris Plages
- Parc Floral
- Parc de la Villette Palais-Royal
- Parc Monceau
- Parc Montsouris
- TGV (train à grande vitesse)
- The Alwyne Castle
- Tour Eiffel
- Tour Montparnasse

Bibliography

I read different books as part of my research. Some of them together with other references include:

The Artist Way - **Julia Cameron**
The Complete Reader - **Neville Goddard**, compiled and
edited by **David Allen**
Psycho-Cybernetics - **Maxwell Maltz**
A Theory of Human Motivation - **Abraham Maslow**

Printed in Great Britain
by Amazon

83051900R00031